The Witch Who Couldn't Spell

Jonathan Allen

ORCHARD BOOKS

ORCHARD BOOKS
96 Leonard Street, London EC2A 4RH
Orchard Books, Australia
14 Mars Road, Lane Cove, NSW 2066
1 85213 887 4 (hardback)
1 86039 068 4 (paperback)
First published in Great Britain in 1995
First paperback publication 1996
Copyright © Jonathan Allen 1995
The right of Jonathan Allen to be identified as the author and
illustrator of this work has been asserted by him in accordance
with the Copyright, Designs and Patents Act, 1988
A CIP catalogue record for this book is available
from the British Library.
Printed and bound in Great Britain
by The Guernsey Press Company Ltd.

Contents

Here Comes Trouble...

A long time ago there lived a very famous wizard called Grimweed. His potions were so popular and worked so well that he was known as "The Mighty Grimweed, King of Potions". People came great distances to consult him personally, or just to make use of his revolutionary While-U-Wait potion service. As wizards go, he was definitely a bit special.

On the morning I want to tell you about, Grimweed was enjoying a few private moments in the garden, pruning his roses. He was very proud of his roses. And justifiably so, because only last year they had won him first prize at the local garden show. He was almost more proud of that achievement than he was of being voted number one in the Wiz Bizz for a record thirteenth year running at this year's three Ws conference. (Three Ws stands for Wizards, Witches, Warlocks and allied Magic Practitioners. Every year they have a special conference where they make speeches and give out awards, voting for the best magic-maker in the business.)

You see, Grimweed's roses were grown without the benefit of magic. Wizards get a special thrill out of succeeding at something without having to use magic – it makes them feel . . . well, more human somehow.

He was just getting to grips with a particularly unruly climbing specimen when he noticed a strange smell. He stopped his pruning and sniffed. Phew! It wasn't just strange, it was extremely unpleasant and, what's more, it was getting stronger. He looked around. Where on earth was it coming from? Had there beeen an unscheduled manure delivery? No, no manure ever smelt *this* bad! As he turned his head, he caught sight of a black shape in the sky. He

looked up. Whatever it was, it was approaching at considerable speed. The smell was growing stronger too. Grimweed shaded his eyes and squinted at the shape.

"A broomstick!" he said to himself. "Well, well, I wonder who's flying it because whoever it is, they're going to miss the landing strip on the south turret by miles at this rate! In fact," he added, edging towards the shelter of the coal bunker, "I think they're going to crash!"

Lloyd joined him.

"What's goig od?" he asked, holding his nose, "and whad's thad horrigle sbell?"

"No time for explanations now," said Grimweed hurriedly, grabbing Lloyd's arm. "There's a low-flying witch coming in at high speed! I don't know about you, but I'm getting out of the way!"

So saying, Grimweed dived behind the coal-bunker. Lloyd followed, and not a moment too soon! There was a "Whoosh". A high, cackly voice cried "Gangwaaay!", then "Aaargh!" and "Ooogh!" as a series of thumps and crashes shook the ground. This was followed by a loud tearing noise and a final "Urgh!"

Lloyd flinched as a battered pointy hat bounced over the coal-bunker and lodged itself in the rose bush behind him. Grimweed reached back and pulled it free. He peered at it. Just inside the rim was written, "Elspeth McGurn, Wicked Witch of the West, by Appointment".

"Old Elspeth," he muttered, getting to his feet. So that's who it is. I do hope she's all right. I wonder what brings her here, and if it's got anything to do with that diabolical smell." By now the stench had become unbearable.

"Aaooh!" groaned Elspeth McGurn, Wicked Witch of the West, as Grimweed and Lloyd helped her out of the remains of a large rose bush. "Ooourgh! Not one of my better landings. Still, I'm out of practice."

Once clear of the last of the thorns, she stood up and looked round.

"Grimweed!" she cried, snatching her hat back from his grasp and jamming it on her head. "Just the man I wanted to see!"

"Elspeth," said Grimweed, when he was sure that there were no bones broken, and that she really was all right. "What brings you here in such a hurry? And what on earth is making that unbelievable smell? They'll be able to smell it in Fabanga!"*

"Don't ask!" cried Elspeth, throwing up her hands. "Don't ask!"
"I've got some Grimproductz Extra-Strength Magic Deodorant you could use," interrupted Grimweed, "but I think it would be out of its depth with that pong."

* Fabanga is a small country on the other side of the Bogle Sea — i.e. a long way away.

Elspeth glared at him.

"It's not me that smells, you stupid Wizard!" she exclaimed indignantly, giving Grimweed a petulant slap on the arm. "It's that thing over there!" She waved her hand at the remains of the rose bush. "And don't interrupt me!"

"Sorry," Grimweed apologized. He peered into the tangled branches where Elspeth had crash-landed. "What old thing?" he asked.

"My broom-stink!" cried Elspeth.

"Your WHAT?" said Lloyd and Grim-weed together.

"My broom-STINK," repeated Elspeth slowly. Grimweed and Lloyd looked at each other.

"Er . . . shouldn't that be 'broom-STICK?'" asked Lloyd, then immediately wished he hadn't.

Elspeth glared at him. "Of course it should be broom-STICK!" she cried. "Of course it should be! That's the whole point! If it was a broom-STICK, I wouldn't be here! What a stupid question! I've turned grown men into . . . into . . . aardvarks for asking questions like that!"

"Er, Elspeth!" interjected Grimweed, in a calming tone of voice. "Forgive me for saying so, but you didn't come here just to turn my staff into exotic animals, although in some cases it might be an improvement." He winked at Lloyd, who was looking somewhat worried. "You obviously have some kind of problem which requires my assistance. Come into my office and tell me exactly what's been going on, calmly and slowly, over a nice cup of tea. You must be tired after your long journey."

"Don't patronize me, young Trevor Wilson!" snapped Elspeth waving a bony finger. "I remember you when you were still in magic nappies! But I'll have a cup of tea all the same."

Still muttering and grumbling, she allowed Grimweed to show her into his office and sit her down while he sent for some tea. When she was a bit calmer, Grimweed beckoned to Lloyd, who approached nervously.

"Lloyd, get some of the apprentices down here and tell them to put a Smell-No-More spell on that broom-stink, will you? If they can't manage that, tell them to put it in the old dungeon and I'll see to it later. And Lloyd," he added, as Lloyd turned to go, "don't worry about Elspeth. She's a bit crotchety at times but she doesn't mean anything by it. She is a *wicked* witch after all."

"What's that you're saying?" said Elspeth suspiciously. "Muttering behind my back!"

"I'm just telling Lloyd that you're a bad-tempered old so-and-so who never stops moaning!" replied Grimweed in a loud voice.

"Fair comment!" said Elspeth, with the beginnings of a grin. "That's why I'm a wicked witch and not one of those do-goody types like you, Grimweed!"

"See what I mean?" said Grimweed.

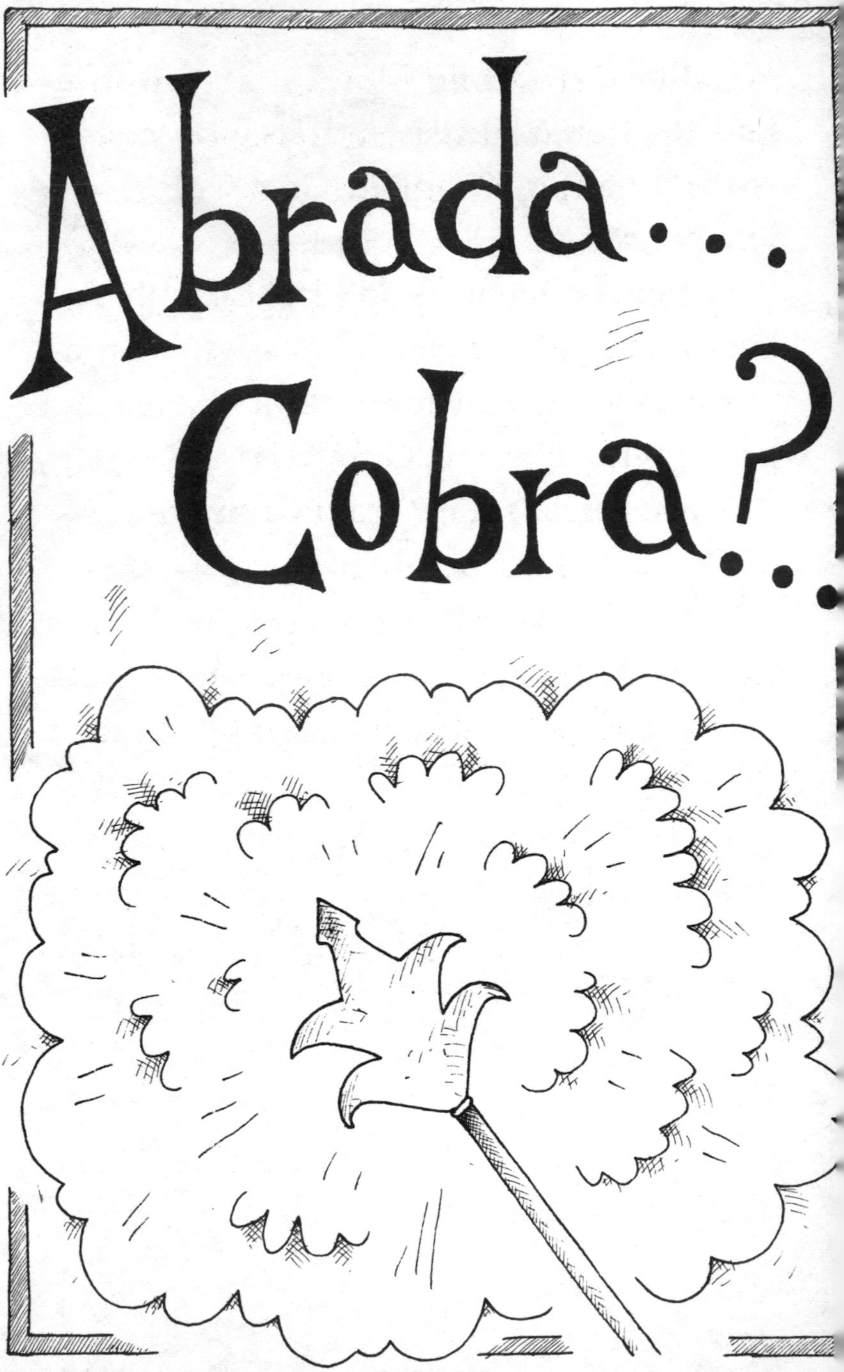
Abrada...
Cobra?..

Outside Grimweed's office a group of apprentice wizards and witches stood around the broom-stink trying out their Smell-No-More spells (not an easy spell to recite while holding your nose!), while inside Elspeth told Grimweed and Lloyd a very strange story indeed.

"It all started when I decided to move house," she began. "You see, trade was picking up and I had to have more room. All sorts of people were coming to do business with me. My curses, spells and incantations were becoming the talk of the kingdom. I even had a successful sideline in home-made jam. Everything was looking rosy until I decided to move."

"That mysterious cave you worked from had a lot of character," said Grimweed. "Good, solid Wicked Witch stuff, I thought."

"Yes, but it was so small," replied Elspeth. "Not to mention damp and uncomfortable, and at my age, character is no substitute for somewhere nice and warm to put your feet up. So I thought I'd go for the traditional Wicked Witch look. What I really fancied was a Gingerbread House!"

"Ooh, yes!" exclaimed Grimweed. "Very traditional! Except I've heard that mice can be a problem and blackbirds, not to mention small children. . ."

"I found the perfect location," Elspeth continued, ignoring Grimweed's interruptions. Right at the edge of a deep, dark wood with gnarled old trees, screech owls, bats, the lot. I had the colour of the curtains and carpets all worked out and, best of all, I had this wonderful Gingerbread House spell which had been handed down from my great-grandmother. Everything was set. So I cast the spell, waved my wand and POW! there it was!"

"Your Gingerbread House?" asked Lloyd.

"Not exactly," replied Elspeth. "Not exactly. It wasn't a Ginger-BREAD house as such, what I actually got was a Ginger-BEARD house!"

Lloyd gasped and Grimweed raised one eyebrow.

"What did it look like?" asked Lloyd. "I bet it looked really weird!"

"It certainly did!" agreed Elspeth. "It looked like a house, only one made out of coarse, curly red hairs with bits of dinner stuck to them. It looked pretty peculiar, I can tell you. But I had to move into it all the same — I had nowhere else to go. Besides, it was warm and kept the rain out. The biggest problem was that the hair kept growing. Imagine living in a house where you have to trim the walls with a pair of

shears every three weeks!"

"Phew!" said Lloyd.

"And that was just the beginning!" Elspeth went on, warming to her theme. "I tried some home improvements to make the place more Wicked-Witch-like, and soon wished I hadn't. For instance, I decided that the front door should make a proper, mysterious creak when you opened it. Nice and spooky! That always goes down well with customers. So I cast the spell, waved my wand and POW! What do you think I got? A mysterious creak? I rushed over and opened the door. No chance! I got a mysterious CROAK instead! It was a disaster! If my customers found out, they'd die laughing and my reputation would be in tatters!"

"Hmm, I see what you mean," said Grimweed sympathetically. "But I still don't understand where the smell comes in."

"Don't be so impatient!" scolded Elspeth. "I haven't told you about the sign."

"The sign?" said Lloyd.

"I wanted to make a magic sign for the front gate," Elspeth continued, "to attract passing trade and let people know they were at the right house. It was going to say simply:

'Here lives the Wicked Witch of the West' in magic luminous writing. But the first time I tried the sign-writing spell I got:

HERE LIES THE WINKLE WENCH OF THE WAST

'Here lies the Winkled Wench of the Waste'. That was no good, so I tried again, and got:

'Hear leaves the Whickered Winch and Her Vest.'

It was useless. Eventually I gave up and wrote it out by hand."

She shook her head sadly. "Those weren't the only strange things that happened," she went on. "One day there was a knock at the door. Well, you know how there's always some would-be hero who wants to come round and chop off the Wicked Witch's head?"

Grimweed groaned and nodded. "Wizards get this problem too," he said. "It's most annoying. I blame all those cheap magic swords on the market nowadays."

"That's right!" said Elspeth. "Well, I had one of those magic-sword boys at my front door. 'Hello, you must be the wicked witch. Do you mind if I chop your head off?' he said, the idiot. Well, I turned him into a frog straight away, no messing! Only it didn't quite work out like that."

"What happened?" asked Lloyd.

"Suddenly the air round the front door was filled with a strange mist that wasn't there before," said Elspeth mysteriously. "I'd turned him into a FOG, hadn't I!" She paused for effect. Lloyd whistled.

"I mean it's just as effective but still not what I'd intended," she continued. "Well, as you can imagine, by now business was not good. I daren't use my magic in public because I didn't know what I was going to end up with. I was running out of excuses. If it hadn't been for my wart cure, I don't know what I would have done."

"I'm glad something turned out right for you," said Lloyd.

Elspeth looked a bit embarrassed.

"Well, it didn't come out quite how I expected. Er, . . . it doesn't exactly cure *warts*. It cures something a bit more anti-social, if you see what I mean. Er, um . . ." She coughed, "but it's very effective, and

one of the most popular things I've done . "

"I see . . . " said Lloyd.

"Eh?" said Grimweed, puzzled.

"Change the first letter!" whispered Lloyd.

"Art . . Bart . . Cart . ." mouthed Grimweed. "Dart . . Eart . . F . . Ah! I see what you mean. Ahem!"

"I was so desperate," continued Elspeth, "I even tried some Fairy-Godmothering. There's always work for Fairy Godmothers, I said to myself. So I did a bit of practice to get my hand in, so to speak. I got hold of a pumpkin, and looked up one of those Fairy Godmother spells — 'How to turn a pumpkin into a coach', that sort of thing. Well, I recited the spell, waved my wand and POW! It turned into a *couch* instead! It was a nice,

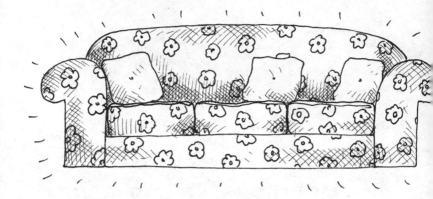

comfortable couch, but it wasn't what I was after. I obviously had a very serious problem. It was then that I decided to come to you, Grimweed."

"Very wise," said Grimweed. "I'm just glad you didn't try to turn mice into horses to pull the coach — you might have ended up with a couch and four HOUSES!" he chuckled.

"Or four HOSES" put in Lloyd. "But seriously, what about that smell?"

"Ha, ha," said Elspeth, "very funny. Well, if you're going to treat my problem like some silly word game, you can work it out for yourselves!" snapped Elspeth.

"Sorry," said Grimweed.

Lloyd thought for a while. "I know," he said at last. "You wanted to turn an ordinary broom into a magic broomstick and got a magic broom-*stink* instead!"

"Spot on!" cried Elspeth. "Maybe I won't turn you into an aardvark after all! Maybe just a pygmy anteater."

Can a Spell Spell?

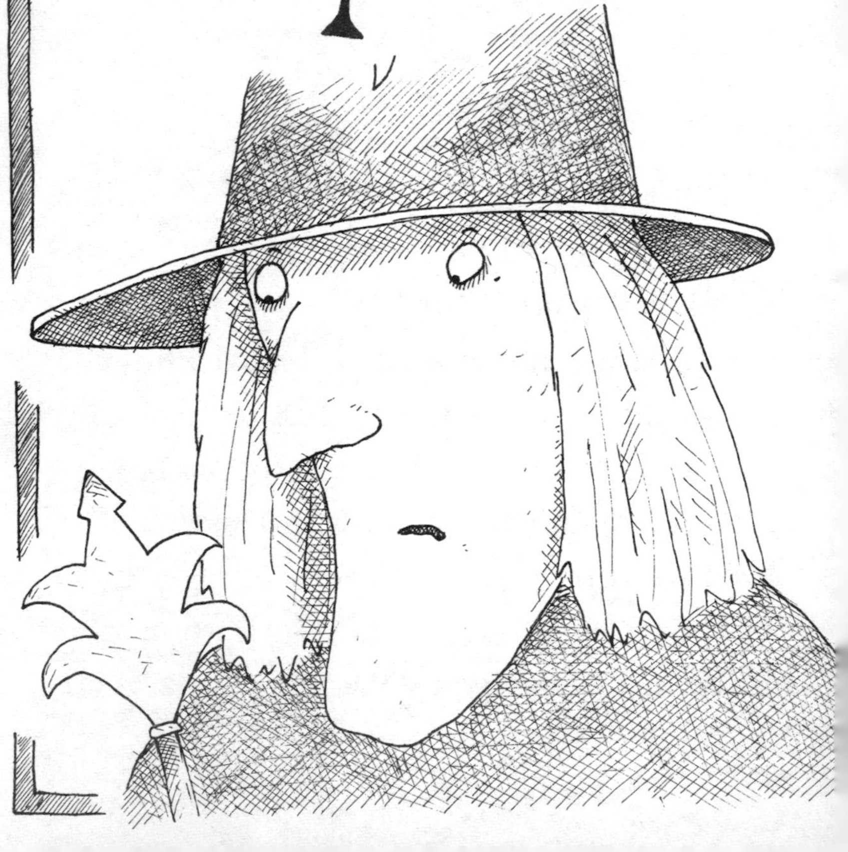

Grimweed looked thoughtful. "It's as if your spells can't spell," he said.

"That's right!" agreed Elspeth. "Every spell turns into misspell, if you see what I mean. I was hoping you might be able to tell me why."

"What kind of wand do you use?" he asked, at length. "Do you mind if I have a look at it?"

"Certainly not," said Elspeth, reaching into her witches' travelling bag. "It's an old thing but I'm very fond of it. It belonged to my grandmother."

Grimweed took the wand carefully.

"Wow," he gasped. "That is an old one and no mistake. Lloyd, what do you make of this?"

Lloyd whistled.

"It looks like a Wimble and Hump 'B' series Mark Two to me," he said, examining the end. "With a type-F rustic handle, if I'm not mistaken. This is a collector's item!"

"It's actually a type-C handle with an F modification added later," Grimweed corrected him. "Look at the spacing."

"Oh yeah," said Lloyd peering even more closely. "Charlie would love this!"

"Charlie is our wand technician," Grimweed explained to Elspeth. "He knows everything there is to know about wands. Tell me," he asked, "when did you last have it serviced?"

"Eh?" said Elspeth.

"Serviced, you know, looked at by a qualified wand technician," said Grimweed.

"Er, not recently," said Elspeth.

"How recently?" asked Grimweed.

"Er, never," volunteered Elspeth. "I've not seen the need," she continued haughtily. "Neither did my mother, or her mother before her."

"I see," said Grimweed. "So you've never been in for the special three Ws ten-point wand check, even though it's done free of charge, and you don't have an official wand-holder's logbook?"

Elspeth shook her head.

"Hmmm," continued Grimweed. "It's important to keep your wand up to scratch, you know," he lectured her. "If a wand isn't serviced at least every thirty years, it can get unpredictable to say the least. Yours seems to have gone wildly out of alignment. I would advise that you have it looked at very soon or it will get even worse."

"What?" cried Elspeth. "Granny's wand? Gone funny? I take it that's what you mean. Are you sure? I've never had any trouble with it and neither did my mother or her mother before her."

"Well, if you don't believe me," said Grimweed, "I suggest you try an experiment. Do some simple magic using a different wand — mine for instance — and see if it comes out right. If it does, well, you can draw your own conclusions, but I'd say all the signs point to something being badly wrong with your wand."

"And if it doesn't come out right, it means there's something badly wrong with me, I suppose!" said Elspeth. "All right, I'll give it a try. Chuck us your wand and I'll see what I can do."

Grimweed handed his wand to her.

"You'll find it rather different from your old thing," he told her.

"You're not wrong!" said Elspeth, grabbing Grimweed's wand and waving it around. "These modern lightweight things! How can you do proper magic with a flimsy piece of apparatus like this?"

"I shall ignore that," said Grimweed, good humouredly. "Wicked Witches don't know about such things as subtlety. You're obviously accustomed to using something the size and weight of a pickaxe handle, and about as gentle."

Elspeth snorted.

"Look," suggested Grimweed. "I've got an idea. Why don't you turn that glass paperweight into a crystal ball? That would be useful, and should be fairly risk-free. If the spell works, I can call Charlie our wand man and ask him his opinion."

"Don't remind me!" groaned Elspeth. "I forgot to tell you. But I tried that spell at home last week. The trouble was I ended up with a crystal *bell!* The second time I tried, I got a crystal *bull.* Very decorative, but not much use to anybody. But anyway, here goes!"

She stood back, struck an attitude and muttered a few strange-sounding words, finishing the performance with a dramatic wave of her, or rather, Grimweed's wand. There was a flash, a plume of purple smoke, and the paperweight was no longer there. Instead, was a perfect crystal ball.

"Hmmmm," said Elspeth. "Not a misspelling in sight, so to speak. It looks like you might be right, Grimweed, more's the pity. She frowned and gave Grimweed's wand a swish. "Granny's wand!" she muttered. "Up the creek! Who would have thought it!"

She looked at Grimweed and sighed.

"Go on, then. Call your blooming wand man. You win!"

Wand Worries Worsen

Even in miniature, viewed via the crystal ball, Charlie's face was not a happy one. "Spelling problems on a Mark Two." He shook his head gravely. "Even with the F-mode on the handle, it sounds serious. I'd better come down."

"Doesn't it just need a service?" asked Grimweed, as Charlie entered the room. "Well, I'm not saying that a service wouldn't help," Charlie acknowledged, "but when you get a Mark Two that old, it's the other things that can go wrong that worry me." He picked up the wand and held it to the light.

"Like what?" asked Grimweed. "Complete Magical Breakdown? Magic Overload Syndrome?"

"Not so much those," said Charlie. "I was thinking worse things than that. Seeing as nobody's checked that wand for well over thirty years, it's the possibility of *infestation* that worries me . . . "

Grimweed's face fell. "Oh no! You don't mean . . . "

"Magic Mites!" said Charlie. "It sounds to me like the magical core has been damaged. Magic Mites can do that if left undisturbed." He looked at the wand through his magnifying glass and shook his head. "Oh dear," he said. "Oh dear, oh dear!"

"Let's have a look," said Grimweed. "Oh no!" He shut his eyes and made an anguished gesture. "Magic Mites!" he groaned. "I thought we'd done for them thirty years ago!"

"Magic Mites?" echoed Lloyd. "Did you say Magic mites? They were supposed to have been wiped out!"

"They were," replied Grimweed. "But certain people who didn't bother to have their wands checked have been harbouring a small colony of them for years, it would seem."

"Magic Mites?" cried Elspeth, jumping up. "Not a chance! My mother used to rub that wand with a piece of garlic sausage every night without fail, to guard against Magic Mites, and so do I . Magic Mites wouldn't go near it!"

"And to think I actually handled that disgusting object," said Grimweed, pulling a face. "Whatever your mother did, Elspeth, I'm sorry to say that it didn't work. Have a look through this magnifying glass."

Elspeth leaned forward and peered into the lens.

"I don't see anything . . . Ah . . . Oh dear! . ."

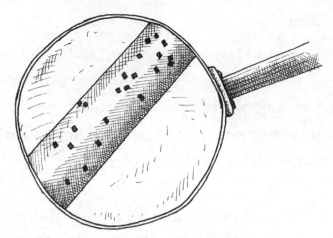

The wand's handle was pitted with tiny holes, tiny square holes. Well, they were Magic Mites.

(Magic Mites, for those of you who weren't around in the Great Mite Crisis of thirty years ago, are a magical version of woodworm, but they don't just eat wood. They eat anything that's been in contact with magic: wands, pointy hats, cloaks, and especially magic books. They became so numerous in those years that the whole magic profession was thrown into turmoil. Luckily, the young Grimweed, aided by his tutor, Wizard Bootspittle the Third, invented a potion which effectively dealt with them. It was called "Mite-No-More" and was the start of Grimweed's brilliant career. Within six months the Magic Mite was wiped out. Or so everyone thought .)

"What happens now?" asked Elspeth, looking suitably worried.

"Normally, what would happen is that you and your wand would have to be decontaminated," said Charlie.

"Not just you and your wand," added Grimweed," but also anybody who's been in contact with your wand — they could be carrying Magic Mites in their clothing or their hair or on their hands. They have to be decontaminated too."

"The trouble is," said Lloyd, looking worried, "because it's been so long since anybody needed it, there's no Mite-No-More potion in the storeroom. I know because I did the stocktaking last week and I'm sure I would have noticed any really old bottles lying around."

"What! None?" cried Grimweed. "What do we do now? I might be able to make up a small amount from the ingredients I've got in store, but I couldn't make enough to decontaminate Elspeth's house, us lot, this room and the broom-stink. I'd need gallons! If we're not

careful, we could have another epidemic on our hands!"

"We'll have to magic-proof this room," said Charlie, "and stay here until we can get some more raw materials in. It could take a month, but it's the only way!"

"A month!" gasped Elspeth. "I'm not staying in one room for a month with a bunch of wizards and a broom-stink!"

"I could do a Go-to-Sleep-for-a-Month potion," suggested Grimweed. "That way we wouldn't get on each other's nerves."

"That may not be necessary," said Lloyd. "I've got an idea. Look, can you give me five minutes?"

"All right," said Grimweed, guardedly. "But what's the big secret?"

"You'll see!" said Lloyd, as he hurried out.

"He's a good lad," said Grimweed, after Lloyd had gone. "I taught him everything he knows, of course, but I haven't a clue what he's up to."

He didn't have to wait long to find out. There was a clanking noise and Lloyd pushed his way into the room, carrying a large bucket of grey liquid, and a garden spray.

"How do you know when Magic Mites are dead?" he asked.

"They give off blue smoke, and sometimes the odd flash of blue flame," said Grimweed. "If that's what I think it is, it's worth a try, but I don't hold out much hope. Go on, though. Let's see what happens."

"What is that stuff?" asked Elspeth.

"It's a special mixture for getting rid of mites on my roses," said Grimweed. "But it's not in the least big magic."

"May I?" asked Lloyd, picking up Elspeth's wand and holding it over the bucket.

"Go on, then," said Elspeth. "It can't be worse than garlic sausage." Lloyd dipped the end of the wand in the bucket, held it there for a minute, then pulled it out. They all gathered round excitedly.

"What's happening?" asked Lloyd. "Come on Charlie. Any blue smoke?"

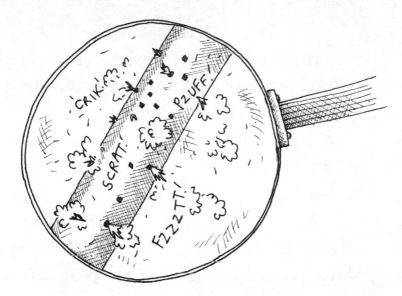

"Not as yet . . ." said Charlie, peering through the magnifying glass. "Not as yet . . . Ooooh!" He jerked his head back as the wand made a crackling noise and a series of small blue flames burst out of the Magic Mite holes. Blue smoke began to snake up into the room.

"Yes," cried Grimweed. "Well done, Lloyd! To think that thirty years ago old Bootspittle and I nearly wore ourselves to a shadow trying to find a magic potion to kill those mites, when all we needed was some rose-mite spray!"

"To be fair," said Lloyd, "it is your special recipe rose-mite spray, and that didn't exist thirty years ago."

"True," said Grimweed, relieved," but it only goes to show that being a wizard isn't just about magic."

"Right!" he continued, "if you could give us all the once-over with that spray, Lloyd, we can see about making up a few gallons more. We've got some decontaminating to do!"

chapter 4½: Back To Normalit

So the crisis was over. The hard work wasn't, though, and for the rest of the day Grimweed and Lloyd, aided by the other apprentices, decontaminated anything and everything that might have come into contact with the Magic Mites. A special hit squad was sent out (on the now odourless broom-stink) to give Elspeth's Ginger-beard House a good going over, while her wand lay soaking in a tank of rose-mite spray.

"Well!" said Grimweed, putting his spray-gun down, "that should do it. It's safe to use magic again, now." (It was considered unwise to use magic near Magic Mites because they absorbed it, and that made them start to reproduce . . .)

"It's worth making sure we've always got a reasonable quantity of rose-mite spray in store in case something like this happens again," said Lloyd, sensibly.

"Absolutely," said Grimweed, "and to be on the safe side, I'm going to make a light weight Test-your-own-Wand kit for the witch and wizard on the move, including a trial-sized sachet of Magic Mite spray, just in case there are any more Magic Mites out there. It should sell well. I'm going to call it Grimweed and Lloyd's Mite buster!"

"My name on the cover!" cried Lloyd. "Yeah! Nice one! Thanks, Grimweed." He paused, then nudged Grimweed in the ribs. "But shouldn't that be Lloyd and Grimweed's Mite-Buster?!"

"Watch it!" said Grimweed, smiling. "No, it shouldn't. Incidentally, where's Elspeth?"

"She was in the lab, with Charlie last time I saw her," replied Lloyd. "Talking wands. They were engrossed in the wand catalogue."

"Well, Elspeth," Grimweed heard Charlie say as he walked into the Magic lab, "this one is probably better than the Mark Five for your purposes, but I'm afraid it doesn't come in a turquoise metallic finish. He pointed to a picture in the wand catalogue on the table in front of them.

"But you can do the mauve suede handle?" asked Elspeth, anxiously. "And I'll want the travelling case as well."

"No problem," said Charlie. "We can have that ready for you by Thursday week at the latest . . . Oh, hello, Grimweed."

"Hello Charlie. Hello Elspeth," said Grimweed. "What's up?"

"I'm ordering a new wand," said Elspeth defiantly, "just in case my old one is damaged beyond repair. These modern wands are not to my taste, as you know . . . er, um . . ."

"Of course not," said Grimweed, suppressing a grin. "The very idea! Anyway, what I came up here to say was, I hope everything is to your satisfaction. I'm glad we could be of assistance to you in your time of trouble."

Elspeth grinned. "Well, it sticks in my throat to say it, me being a Wicked Witch and all," she said. "But, thank you, Grimweed, and thanks to Lloyd too. Tell him I'm not going to turn him into anything and that he's welcome to visit my ginger-BREAD house anytime he likes. That goes for you too, of course."

"I'd be delighted," said Grimweed. "Now, you must excuse me, I've got some work to do, but I'm sure Charlie will give you the very best advice."

"Of course, there's the ultra-light-weight Turbo version," continued Charlie, when Grimweed had left the room. "But that might be a bit too sporty for you . . ."

"Too sporty for me?" cried Elspeth, peering at the catalogue. "Impossible!"

Jonathan Allen lives in Hertfordshire with his wife, Marian, their small daughter, Isobel, and his cat, William. When not writing or drawing, he likes eating, birdwatching, listening to and playing music.

BEST WISHES ..... Jonathan

The Witch Who Couldn't Spell